Monty and the Pudding
Written by Gayle Clarke

Wee Mackay Publishing

Also available in the Monty series:

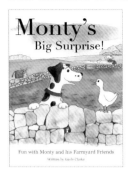

Monty's Big Surprise!

First published 2013 by Wee Mackay Publishing
21 Kessington Square, Bearsden, Glasgow G61 2QQ

ISBN: 978-0-9570946-1-1

©Text 2013 Gayle Clarke
©Illustrations 2013 Martin Teviotdale

Edited by Gale Winskill
www.winskilleditorial.co.uk

Illustrations by Martin Teviotdale
www.teviotdale-illustration.co.uk
Printed in Great Britain

www.weemackaypublishing.co.uk

Monty looked at a bone, but then had a better idea ... or so he thought. "I will take jelly and ice cream," he announced.

The others looked at each other in disbelief.

"Don't be silly, Monty," said Bubbles. "Jelly and ice cream will melt in the sun, and besides, dogs don't like jelly and ice cream."

"Well, I do!" said Monty. "You'll see. It will be fine."

As the animals were about to head off, they saw the farmer talking to someone.

Monty looked over and there, to his surprise, was a Collie puppy.

"Look," said the farmer, "I've brought you a friend. You can share your dinner and your bed with the puppy."

"I'm not sharing anything with him," said Monty.

"*He* is a *she*," laughed the farmer, "and I thought you might like to choose a name for her."

"*She* doesn't need a name," said Monty, and he ran off to join the other animals.

The puppy raced behind, trying hard to keep up.

They hadn't gone very far when, sure enough, the jelly and ice cream started to soften in the sun.

The jelly wobbled and slobbled and blobbled, all over the place.

And the ice cream slurped and blurped, and ran down Monty's face.

"I told you that would happen, Monty," said Bubbles rather smugly, "but you wouldn't listen."

Feeling rather hungry, the animals decided to have their picnic.

All, that is, except Monty, who thought he would save his until later.

The puppy looked longingly at the jelly and ice cream, but Monty ignored her.

Suddenly, a strange noise came from the bushes.
   Monty and his friends peered into the darkness and there, curled up in five little balls, were five ducklings.
   "We've lost our mummy," they cried. "We were playing and wandered away from her."

"Never mind," said Monty, "I have an idea."

"Oh, here we go again!" said Splasher. "Another idea from Monty!" But sometimes Monty did have good ideas.

"You can come home with us," he said. "Each one of you can give five feathers and we will leave a trail, which your mummy can follow when she's looking for you."

The ducklings thought that was a great plan.

"Right, each of us will carry one of you on our back," said Monty in a rather bossy voice.

But in turn the animals said, "I'm not sharing my back with a duckling. They've got dirty feet."

"Well then," said Monty, "I'll carry all the ducklings on my back. But it's good to share, you know."

"I could help," said the puppy, anxiously wanting to please.

"You're too small," scoffed Monty.

As the ducklings climbed on to Monty's back they began to slide about, because … the jelly wobbled and slobbled and blobbled, all over the place.

And the ice cream slurped and blurped, and ran down Monty's face.

"We told you that would happen, Monty," said Sammy smugly, "but you wouldn't listen."

"All aboard!" shouted Monty and they set off, leaving the trail of feathers behind them.

The ducklings laughed and tried to avoid the dripping jelly and ice cream.

Monty was quite hungry now, but most of his picnic had melted, leaving a sloppy mess all over his back.

The ducklings giggled as they slid about.

After a long, hot journey, the animals arrived back at the farm, exhausted.

Monty helped the ducklings off his back and they fell asleep immediately, in a corner of the yard.

Suddenly, Monty heard the puppy yapping
and, looking up, he saw a large brown duck
talking to her.

"Who are you? That's my puppy," said Monty in a very unsharing sort of way.

"I'm Matilda," said the duck, "and I've lost my ducklings. I told them to stay close. I've been searching for hours, then I found a trail of their feathers which led to this farm. Have you seen my ducklings?"

"Yes!" cried Monty.

At that moment, there was a commotion and the ducklings came rushing over, shouting, "Mummy! Mummy! We're so sorry. We were playing and wandered away from you, even though you told us to stay nearby!"

"Well, you'll know next time," she said kindly. "Now, let's go home."

Monty felt rather lonely as the ducklings waddled off.

The puppy watched Monty as he tried to wipe the gooey mess from his face. She wanted so much to be his friend and she started to jump up and down, trying to attract his attention. But Monty ignored her.

Well, she thought, there must be something
I can do to cheer Monty up.

She ran over and started licking Monty's face frantically, so much so that she got in quite a state and her little tongue was rather sore.

Monty giggled. It was quite tickly having his face licked and, before they even realised, the two were playing together, having great fun.

"Well," said Monty, "this is wonderful having another new friend to play with. I'm sorry I was mean to you. I didn't let you join in with our fun, and I didn't share my picnic either."

"Well, you're sharing it now," she laughed, licking the very last trace of ice cream and jelly until ... there was no more jelly to wobble and slobble and blobble, all over the place.

And no more ice cream to slurp and blurp, and run down Monty's face.

Just then, the other animals arrived with the farmer, in time to see Monty and the puppy playing happily together.

The farmer was delighted to see that the puppy had settled in so well, and that Monty had found his kind heart and welcomed her after all.

"We didn't think that would happen," he said, smiling.

"You know," said Monty, "maybe I will share my bed and my food with the puppy. I could even give her a name. I could call her Pudding!"

And they all laughed and felt very happy indeed.